Potato Chip Books

SO GOOD YOU CAN'T STOP READING THEM!

Let's Run

Written by John Bianchi & Jane Hileman
Illustrated by John Bianchi

Let's go for a run.

We'll run around the table.

We'll run and
jump over the cat.

We'll run up the stairs.

We'll run over here and look in the mirror.

We'll run under the bed.

We'll run down the stairs.

We'll run over to Dad and give him a kiss.

We'll run over to Mom and give her a kiss, too.

Let's go for a walk.